this
little  ORCHARD
book belongs to

....

....

For Hamish T.P.

ORCHARD BOOKS
96 Leonard Street, London EC2A 4XD
Orchard Books Australia
32/45-51 Huntley Street, Alexandria NSW 2015
1 84362 221 1
First published in Great Britain in 2000
This edition published in 2003
Illustrations © Penny Dann 2000
The right of Penny Dann to be identified as
the illustrator of this work has been asserted by her
in accordance with the Copyright, Designs and Patents Act, 1988.
A CIP catalogue record for this book is available from the British Library.
Printed in Italy

Five in the bed

Penny Dann

little ORCHARD

There were five in the bed,
And the little one said,

Roll over, roll over!

They all rolled over,
And one fell out
Then gave a little shout.

So there were four in the bed,
And the little one said,

Roll over, roll over!

They all rolled over,
And one fell out
Then gave a little shout.

So there were three in the bed,
And the little one said,

They all rolled over,
And one fell out

Then gave a little shout.

So there were two in the bed,
And the little one said,

Roll over, roll over!

They all rolled over,
And one fell out
Then gave a little shout.

So there was one in the bed,
Who turned over and said,

So he stretched and smiled...

Then gave a
BIG shout!